PRAISE FOR THE SERIES

"This book did everything right for me when it comes to what I'm looking for in a fantasy novel. More people need to read this book. Seriously." -SADIR S. SAMIR, AUTHOR OF *THE CREW*

"Excellently written...really ambitious in its craft." -JAMREADS.COM

"Different from typical fantasy novels in all the good ways." -ESCAPIST BOOK CO.

"Emotional and heartbreaking." -JAMES HARWOOD-JONES, GOODREADS REVIEW

"Who could ask for anything more?" -BELINDA RICHEE, GOODREADS REVIEW

"A complete, engrossing story...which packs real emotion and leaves you wanting to find out more." -NICK PROCTOR, GOODREADS REVIEW

"An amazing debut and I can't wait for the follow-up." -AMAZON REVIEW

ALSO BY JOSEPH JOHN LEE

The Spellbinders and the Gunslingers

THE BLEEDING STONE

THE CHILDREN OF THE BLACK MOON

PALE NIGHT, RED FIELDS

A SPELLBINDERS NOVELLA

JOSEPH JOHN LEE

For Andrew

Because a car ran over your foot when you visited while I was writing this

Told you I'd dedicate this to you

CHAPTER ONE

ILL OMENS

THE YEAR 1166 ANNO SALVATORIS
25 YEARS AFTER THE ECLIPSE

The smell of pungent incense hardly mixed well with the pervasive aroma of salt water, but by this point, Zarrow could say he was used to it.

For weeks now, he awoke to the same rituals. Greet the daybreak at the ocean's shore. Procure breakfast from the shallow waters. Indulge his father's recent obsessions with the dead.

On this morning, though, the incense was so rancid that any desire to seek out his daily catch was entirely out of the question. The very thought of food in his stomach was enough to induce nausea in accompaniment with the stench of the hut.

As he lay in bed, Zarrow let loose a deep sigh, running his hands across his face and through the tangled knots of his dark hair, glancing sidelong toward the assembly room of his father's hut.

One cannot speak to the dead if their home does not smell of it, apparently, he thought.

He rose to a seated position, a sudden wave of dense incense sending him into a coughing fit. Tears started to well in his eyes, his lungs burning from the exertion. He winced at the pain in his chest and pushed himself to his feet, damning the fire raging within him. Then, with a shake of his head, he donned his morning robe, an open-chested vestment made of light woven fabric of a plain tanned hue, and tied it at his waist, his pendant thumping against his chest as he walked toward the adjacent room.

Wiping the dampness away from his eyes, he tied his long dark locks back, the end trailing against his back, and spotted his father kneeling before a row of incense candles. More candles than he had ever seen lit at once. *No wonder I can hardly breathe this morning.*

His father was garbed in much more elaborate attire at this hour than he was. As was typical for the shamans of the Tribe, a garish silk robe draped over him, the sleeves open and flowing as he raised his arms in tune with the flickering flames. His hair was tied at the top of his head in a single ponytail while the rest trailed down to the middle of his back. A mask covered his face, almost bearing enough resemblance to his own face, were it instead crafted of oak. A muffled voice ruminated beneath the mask, some sort of prayer made in offering to the gods or the flames. Zarrow was never quite sure to whom the prayers belonged.

Zarrow cleared his throat as he approached, despite the burning sensation from drawing another breath. "Father," he called, wincing at the stench.

His father did not respond, instead remaining attuned to his prayers.

"*Father,*" he repeated, more forcefully this time.

Again, there was no response.

With an annoyed sigh, Zarrow crossed his arms, furrowed his brow, and said, "Shaman Yodir."

Yodir's arms dropped, his prayers quieted. "You forget yourself, my son," he said over his shoulder. "What, may I ask, is of greater importance than my communion with the gods?"

Zarrow coughed again. "My being able to breathe, for starters. Gods, Father, how many of these candles are necessary?"

Yodir rose to his feet, his shaman robe falling past his knees. He towered over Zarrow by at least half a foot, though he remained a rather spindly and lanky man besides. He lifted his mask, revealing a grimacing face slicked with sweat, eyes reddened around his dark irises. He looked at Zarrow down the length of his nose, the elongated curvature of which often gave him a side profile akin to a hawk. "So long as the work continues," he finally said, "the candles are all necessary."

Shaking his head, Zarrow pushed past his father and extinguished the candles one by one. The smell still lingered, but after a few moments, it was not nearly so pervasive and aggressive.

Waving away some residual tufts of smoke, Zarrow turned toward his father's worktable in the corner of the room, a pile of scrambled notes and postulations littering its surface. He picked up a sheet of paper, barely able to decode whatever cipher it was that his father invented beyond understanding what the research was all for.

"Do the dead still wait for your word, then?" he asked, turning his eyes back toward his father.

Yodir scoffed. "You remain dismissive."

"I remain *skeptical*, Father," Zarrow corrected. "I remain *perplexed* at this sudden fascination with the Otherworld."

"You merely lack the dedication."

"More the obsession."

"Then perhaps I have not raised you well enough to know that obsession is, at times, partner to dedication."

Yodir removed his mask entirely and walked toward Zarrow, dropping it unceremoniously on his table. He placed a firm hand on his son's shoulder, the sensation sending a chill down Zarrow's arm. For one so physically unintimidating beyond the height, Zarrow could not help but feel a quiver of apprehension whenever his father drew this close.

"The pursuit of wisdom," Yodir said, "is oft-wrought with obsession."

"You were never this obsessed before," Zarrow said through gritted teeth. "Nor any of the other shamans. It's only within these last weeks that the dead have fascinated you so." He shook his head. "Forgive me if I fail to see the purpose of such pursuits of 'wisdom' as you call them."

The rapping of his father's fingers atop Zarrow's shoulder could very well have been daggers for the sharp chill coursing through him. He rolled his shoulder to release himself from Yodir's grasp, his father willfully obliging before folding his hands behind his back and returning to the unlit candles.

A stark silence gripped the room, broken only by the distant cawing of gulls as they circled the village. Yodir gazed longingly at the ghosts of the candle lights, his eyes not breaking from their memory.

You would seek to commune even with the dead and dying flames, as well, wouldn't you? Zarrow couldn't help but think.

"Perhaps it is my own curse. To have been granted from the Owl his great Knowledge," Yodir murmured. He turned back toward Zarrow, a resolute grimace adorning his face. "It was some weeks ago, during my daily communion with the Owl. It all seemed so simple then..."

Zarrow raised his brow, leaning expectantly. "Simple?" he asked, hoping for some clarification.

A phantom smile curved his father's lips. "There is only so much we may hope to learn in the course of our lives. Only so much knowledge we may hope to gain. When we return ourselves to the earth, with us dies our own knowledge, and we can only remain hopeful as we traverse to the Otherworld that what we have learned is adequately passed down. We are each of us our own living legacies. But the

Otherworld cares not for our legacies or our knowledge or what we pass down. It cares only to allow us...rest."

"But...yes," Zarrow responded in a flat tone. "That is just...life. We live, we die...we rest."

"But what if it need not be so?" Yodir answered, arms flailing triumphantly, a fire suddenly bursting in his eyes. "What if the knowledge we seek would transcend life and death? What if death was not the end but only an extension of ourselves, of our histories? All that we have learned would no longer be limited to our mortal coil but rather to our own tapestry, our own web of knowledge, of culture, of histories and tactics and ideas. We learn from those who came before..." He walked with excitement toward Zarrow, his fingers curling with anticipation. "...by *communing* with those who came before."

Zarrow blinked, the necessary words not finding their way to his lips. It was a protracted silence, one punctuated by sputters and stops on Zarrow's part and expectant, excited breaths on Yodir's. "You...you're..."

Yodir's eyes lit up once more. "Brilliant? A visionary?"

Scoffing, Zarrow shook his head. "Mad." He watched the fire in his father's eyes quell entirely until nothing but smoldering embers remained. "We have tomes for such things, Father! Our people's histories are put to pen and paper. We needn't indulge in—"

A dismissive hand nearly smacked Zarrow in the face. "Paper is not immune to falsehoods, Zarrow," Yodir said. "The pen is subject to the whims of the hand. But were we to listen to those histories given voice, then we—"

"The other shamans agreed with you?" Zarrow interrupted. "They heard your words and decided, 'Yes, this is the path we ought to walk?'"

Yodir pushed past Zarrow, a sly chuckle rumbling in his throat, and picked up a stack of notes that had been strewn across his table.

"Do you presume that mine is the sole hand that drafted these?" He dropped the stack just as unceremoniously, papers scattering in the updraft, pens and inks spilling all along the hut's floor. "It is the responsibility of we shamans to set forth the path that our Tribe is to take."

"It is the responsibility of the shamans to act as a conduit for communion with the gods," Zarrow said flatly. He didn't bother to mask his annoyance at the claim. "What you speak of is—"

"Enough," Yodir said. "We will speak no more of this. So the path is set, and so the Dusk Tribe shall walk it. The work shall continue, and it shan't be long until the gods reveal to us our role in this endeavor." He walked back to the candles and readied the flame to light the incense once more.

Zarrow winced at the impending assault on his nostrils.

"And speaking of which, Zarrow," his father said, fiddling with one of the incense candles before igniting it. "Has your Foresight granted you any insight into our future discoveries?"

Opening his mouth, Zarrow fought back a sudden cough at the fresh smell of incense. He clutched to his pendant, the ornament by which he was granted his abilities as a Futureseer. It had been eight years since he completed his Trial—the coming-of-age ritual through which all Tribespeople pass into adulthood upon reaching their eighteenth year. Being born under the Sign of the Owl meant that Zarrow would eventually be granted a Boon relative to wisdom, much like his father did, and so it happened that Zarrow was one of the rare individuals to be granted the Boon of Foresight. So far as he knew, he was the only Futureseer in the entire Dusk Tribe.

Once his coughing fit subsided, Zarrow managed a shake of the head and squeaked out a meek "No." He cleared his throat and then repeated more clearly, "No, I've not discovered anything, Father."

In truth, Zarrow had not indulged his father's whims on this matter. Scarcely had Zarrow ever felt it necessary to tap into his Foresight and see what was yet to come. He had never developed an interest in those future unknowns, and perhaps that may have been to his father's chagrin.

But on this matter in particular, Zarrow had no desire to seek out just how it would be the Dusk Tribe learned to commune with those who had passed on to the Otherworld, if they discovered it all. But his father would never listen to that reasoning. He knew that. It was simpler to pretend otherwise and hope that these obsessions were merely fleeting.

Regardless, Yodir seemed to accept the answer. He nodded and returned to the incense, lighting the candles one by one before returning to the table to grab his shaman mask. "Continue your search, Zarrow," he said in passing. "Knowing what it will be that we are searching for will be of great assistance to this endeavor." And he knelt back before the candles.

Knowing what will come to pass will not enable it to arrive more quickly, Zarrow was about to say, but a knock at the threshold to the hut interrupted him before he could do so.

A woman cleared her throat in the doorway, peering her head around the corner. "Shaman Yodir? Hello?"

Zarrow and Yodir both craned their heads toward the source of the voice. Immediately, Zarrow recognized her as Verina, one of the Wolfsigns of the Tribe. She was an avid and adept hunter, though he couldn't quite remember what Boon she had been granted upon completing her Trial. He never much interacted with her, but with how small the Dusk Tribe was, everyone knew everyone, at least. Were they of the Stone Tribe, he probably wouldn't have even known she existed.

Upon seeing Verina, Yodir extinguished the incense candles just as quickly as he lit them, removed his mask, and walked over to the woman, quickly beckoning her inside. He clasped her hands softly as she entered, whispering some quiet prayer the words of which Zarrow couldn't quite make out.

A sullen expression was affixed to Verina's face. Her eyes appeared sunken, weathered, with frown lines flanking the edges of her mouth. A loose and unkempt braid of dark hair was draped over her left shoulder, trailing down her informal attire comprised of tanned hides and light leather. As she looked up at Yodir, Zarrow could discern a thinly-veiled expression of resentment and anger in the woman's eyes, interspersed with shades of sadness.

As Yodir concluded his prayer, he clasped Verina's hands more tightly in a gesture that bordered on comforting. "Verina," he said warmly. "Allow me to offer my deepest condolences for your loss. I ask your forgiveness for not having visited you previously."

Verina didn't seem able to rid herself of her frown, but she nodded in acknowledgment just the same.

Zarrow inclined his head at his father's comment, however. "Condolences?" he asked. He took a sheepish handful of steps forward, scratching the back of his head bashfully. "Forgive me, Verina, but you…how do I ask this…?"

The awkwardness of the question seemed to give Verina some minor amusement as she offered a very slight chuckle. "My husband, Sepet. A few days past." She appeared inclined to say more but shut her mouth, shaking her head as though to dam up impending tears.

At first stepping forward to take Verina's hand in an offer of comfort just as his father did, Zarrow instead opted to bow his head, especially once he saw the expression on both Verina and Yodir's faces. Expressions that seemed to imply that his offer was neither requested nor required. Zarrow settled for softly muttering, "My sincerest sympathies, Verina. If there is anything that we can do for you—"

"I would assume now to be the time," Yodir interjected. "If you are visiting at such an early morning hour."

The look in Verina's eyes was all the confirmation that was needed. "Have there been any progress in your attempts to commune with the dead?"

The bluntness of the question took Zarrow by surprise. He did not think that word of the shamans' recent activities had spread through the Tribe so quickly.

From the expression on his father's face, it appeared Yodir had the same thought, but he also seemed much less taken aback by the prompt. If anything, it almost appeared he was relieved to have the opportunity to speak to someone who was so invested in the outcome. Yodir flashed a glance at Zarrow, the shadow of a smirk creasing his lips.

You're excited over this, aren't you? Zarrow thought. *You've found someone with whom to indulge yourself.*

Turning back to Verina, Yodir adopted a comforting smile—one that Zarrow could immediately tell was false—and began to say, "The research into that is ongoing, but we—"

"Sepet was murdered. I intend for him to tell me who did it."

That was enough to quietly wipe the smile from Yodir's face, false though it likely was. It stunned him, even. Zarrow looked to his father and vice versa, both bereft of the words necessary to address the brazen request. The silence lingered for moments that dragged on and on with no noise to break the lingering quiet save for the village's bustling thoroughfares as the Tribe began to wake up.

Though Yodir had quickly adopted an expression of unperturbed stoicism, a twitch of his lips betrayed that motion. Doubt, confusion, they were visible in his eyes. Zarrow had never known his father to be mired in the unknowing. But for there to have been a murder within this Tribe, and none were speaking of it, he couldn't blame his father for such a reaction.

Furrowing his brow, Yodir released his hold on Verina's hands and took a step back, running his fingers through his hair. "Verina, forgive me if I cannot help but wonder what led you to believe that Sepet was—"

"It is not a belief," Verina asserted, crossing her arms. "It is the truth."

"On what basis?" Yodir asked, raising a hand inquisitively. "It was to my understanding that Sepet passed in his sleep. That is not altogether a strange thing."

"For an elder, it is not. Sepet was not an elder. He had seen only thirty-three years, the same as I. Are you saying I should expect to pass in my sleep, as well?"

"It is not merely limited to our elders," Yodir responded, massaging the bridge of his nose between his thumb and forefinger. "Was he at all in poor health? Any instances of—"

"No," Verina was quick to say. "He was the picture of perfect health. There is no reason for him not to have woken from his sleep other than—"

"I am sorry, Verina," Yodir interrupted, raising his hand as a request for her to stop. "But I fail to see what is so suspicious about—"

"It was those Eclipseborn."

Yodir froze, his brow raised. His gaze trailed from one corner of the room to the next, considering the point. "...Ah," he said. And nothing else.

Zarrow could feel his heart sink at the mention of the Eclipseborn. While Tribespeople were typically born under a Sign in relation to one of the three Animal Deities—the Bear, the Wolf, or the Owl—there were, on very rare occasions, children who were born during an

Eclipse and were therefore rejected and unable to participate in their Trials. It was to his understanding that most Tribes would banish the Eclipseborn outright, but there were actually two generations of Eclipseborn who dwelt within the Dusk Tribe's borders, fourteen of them in all. But that never stopped the prejudice. That never stopped the "regular" members of the Tribe from treating the Eclipseborn as "lesser" people or as something to fear.

Despite there being no recorded instances of misfortunes attributed to those born during an Eclipse.

It never made any sense to Zarrow. And it continued to make little sense to him now, especially in watching the tone of his father's voice change entirely. *For a learned man to believe in such superstition...*

Yodir shuffled in place, tapping his foot on the soft flooring below, his forehead wrinkling as he grew deep in thought. "Was there any prior...conflict with any of the Eclipseborn on your husband's part, Verina? Any arguments, altercations, matters of that sort?"

It was all Zarrow could do but shake his head in disbelief.

Verina immediately spat on the ground. "It had to have been that bastard, Tabrum! He always went out of his way to belittle my Sepet! Screaming at him from afar, avoiding him as though he carried a disease. Bless my Sepet, he always sought to be the bigger man, but even *he* grew despondent at such foul treatment. I am *certain* that he confronted Tabrum to the point that that foul man would have wished harm on him!"

You call that cause for suspicion? Zarrow thought.

He had a clear image of Tabrum in his mind. He was a belligerent old man, true, but that was in large part due to his own mistreatment over being born during an Eclipse. Zarrow had never known him to hurt so much as a gadfly.

It seemed enough to convince Yodir, however. A spark glinted in his eyes once again as he pensively stroked his chin. "And you're certain that Tabrum is to blame, then?" he asked.

Verina threw her hands in the air, almost in disbelief. "It could have been any one of those Eclipseborn for all I know! But Tabrum is the worst of them. Why would it *not* be him?"

Yodir wagged an excited finger at her and scurried across the room, shouldering Zarrow out of the way as he rushed for the notes on his desk. Rummaging through the collective scribblings of the Tribe's shamans, he muttered a series of nothings under his breath before emitting a soft chuckle.

Curiosity evident on her face, Verina shuffled out from the doorway and nearer to Yodir's table. "Did you find something, then?"

A wide smile stretched across Yodir's lips as he turned his head over his shoulder. "Stay your grief for now, Verina. It shan't be long before we achieve a breakthrough, I promise you."

Zarrow wondered whether he had time to deconstruct *all* of that, but perplexingly, it seemed to quell Verina's anger enough for her to immediately join Yodir at his table to go over the notes.

And just like that, it was as though Zarrow was hardly a presence in his own home. He felt as though he were a ghost, though if he was, then perhaps *he* was the breakthrough his father had been searching for this whole time.

He couldn't stand to be in this company any further. Not after this continued obsession with the dead, and especially not after the arbitrary blame placed upon the Tribe's Eclipseborn population at large. The village had begun to awaken, and so it seemed a perfect opportunity to greet the morning properly. Wrapping his robe more tightly around his waist, Zarrow exited the hut and out onto the village paths, leaving behind the excited rumblings of a madman and his new confidante.

The mood of the morning aside thus far, it was quite a beautiful day. Finally removed from the lingering pungency of incense, the salt air was a tremendous relief on Zarrow's nose and lungs. As he peered off to the south, he caught a glimpse of the enchanting ocean, its subtle waves beckoning him to enter. Although the sun had only risen not too long ago, it was already growing quite warm. Not too oppressive yet, but it was only a matter of time.

Across the pathway from his hut was the home of his childhood friend, Kaurazi. The door had been left open, a sure sign that Kaurazi was not at home—a habit he still needed to break—but Zarrow had a fair inkling of where he may find his friend. Turning back to the south, he traipsed along the beaten path, rows of huts comprised of clay and hard stone flanking him on either side. At the end of the path, the village's great hall stood tall, a beacon for all points of the Dusk Tribe to converge.

And at this time of the day, they served a fairly hearty breakfast. Kaurazi had never been one to cook for himself, so Zarrow was certain that was where he would be. And now that he had regained his appetite since the incense candles were no longer assaulting his senses, he saw fit to kill two birds with one stone.

The great hall already seemed to be in lively spirits judging from the vibrant din escaping its windows. No matter the time of day, the hall was always the most excitable location in the village. There were no fisheries like he had seen in the Sun Tribe's village, nor large markets as were common amongst the Lake Tribe. It was only here, at this great hall, that the Dusk Tribe socialized, dined, imbibed, and thrived as a cohesive unit.

When Zarrow entered the hall's doors, he drew in deep the wonderful smell of the morning's freshly-cooked catch, enthralling enough to overtake the otherwise musty smell of long wooden tables that had been weighed down by centuries of congealed sweat. Despite the early hours, half the tables were already occupied, and half of those tables' occupants were stuffing their faces. Before seeking out Kaurazi, Zarrow flagged the cook from the other side of the hall, pointed a finger upwards, and waited for an acknowledging grunt before sitting down.

Kaurazi was sat at the edge of a table in the far corner by his lonesome, one of those eager enough to already be eating. Zarrow weaved around several bodies until he found himself standing across from his friend, who was still far too entranced by his food to pay Zarrow any mind.

Zarrow cleared his throat. "Is this seat taken?" he asked, gesturing to the empty spot across from Kaurazi.

Bits of fish dribbled out from Kaurazi's mouth as he grinned and motioned to the vacated bench. "Go righ' ahea'," he said, mouth still filled to the brim with his breakfast.

It was such a stark contrast to how his morning had started that it was hard for Zarrow not to smile. He took his seat across from Kaurazi and patiently awaited his breakfast, which, judging from the plate in front of him, was some combination of fresh fish, steamed carrots, and rice.

"Morning," he said, thumping his thumb against the table in antic- ipation. His stomach was already rumbling.

"Yeah, good mornin'," Kaurazi responded, finally having swallowed his food. "Haven't seen you here for breakfast in a while."

Zarrow shrugged. "Not all that often I get smoked out of the house first thing in the morning."

Kaurazi wrinkled his nose and shook his head. "Was wonderin' why your hut smelled like shit this mornin'. Your father still on this kick of 'talkin' to the dead,' is he?"

"Every day brings a new incense candle for me to gag on. It won't be much longer before the entire village is awoken every morning by the

stench. May we all become better communicants with the gods for it."
He rolled his eyes.

"Can only imagine," Kaurazi said. "Be nice for me to finally get to talk to one of 'em, though. Can't say I'm not curious."

"Trust me, you shouldn't be *that* curious. You might never have an appetite again."

"More coin in my pocket, then. Oh, speakin' o' which." He nudged his head forward. "Looks like your food's here."

Before Zarrow could even look up to the cook to smile in gratitude, the tray was plopped unceremoniously in front of him, nearly thrown at him. The contents sprayed every which way, grains of rice falling through the cracks of the table's wooden slabs and onto the floor.

"Yeah, thanks," Zarrow muttered, not bothering to offer the cook a glance.

The cook muttered something in return, but not audible enough for Zarrow to hear.

Kaurazi smacked his lips, flicking away a few grains of rice that had landed before him. "Been gettin' a lot worse lately, all'a this."

A frown still on his face, Zarrow raised his eyebrows. "All of what?"

"Come on, Zarrow, look around you."

Zarrow obliged, taking note of the empty perimeter surrounding them, all of the other patrons at the great hall sitting far, far away from them, save for one young woman at the table behind Zarrow, her back facing towards his.

"Been seemin' more and more lately that you're the only one who wants anythin' to do with us Eclipseborn," Kaurazi lamented. "Doesn't seem like folks're much happy with you right now, either."

"That's *their* problem, then, isn't it?" Zarrow murmured, picking listlessly at his breakfast which he quickly discovered was under-cooked. "Was I supposed to say 'so long' to a lifelong friendship just because it turned out you're Eclipseborn? I must have missed that memo."

"Ah, the memo was wrongly forged, anyhow," Kaurazi quipped. "Should've read, 'Please be extra nice to the Eclipseborn, you dumb shits.'" He popped another piece of fish into his mouth, and whether *his* was undercooked as well was something Zarrow could not adequately discern. "Point is, you got my gratitude for it. We haven't much wanted to come around here lately. Really just me and Ceverra right behind you."

Zarrow looked over his shoulder at Ceverra, though if she heard her name, she didn't make any inclination to offer a greeting.

"Every once in a while, I might see someone else, but on the regular, it's really just us, and aw shit, what's happenin' over there?"

Following the path of Kaurazi's finger, Zarrow caught sight of two men barking at each other, risen to their feet, though still maintaining a manageable distance. He didn't recognize one of them, but he knew Tabrum's face anywhere. The old Eclipeborn of the generation prior to Kaurazi's cohort had long locks of starkly white hair trailing from the sides of his head, the top housing only sparse, wispy strands of hair. His face was marred with wrinkles and scars alike, his left eye sporting a rather prominent remnant of a brawl marking him from brow to chin.

The two men were screaming at one another, though the exact words were somewhat indistinct over the surrounding commotion. From what Zarrow could tell, however, was that Tabrum was very much red in the face, his voice hoarse, but his hands folded behind his back as he stood several paces away. The man opposite Tabrum was much more animated though nowhere near as distinctive a voice.

But whether the words came from this man or from one of the surrounding onlookers, one phrase that Zarrow could hear repeated several times was, "You don't belong here!"

And before he could process that, Zarrow felt useless as he watched the man take his breakfast plate and heave it with all his strength right at Tabrum's face, the entire payload of fish and rice exploding in the elder Eclipseborn's face. Zarrow winced, covering his shocked, gaping mouth with an open hand. "Gods," he muttered under his breath.

Tabrum grunted but stood his ground, but when a second tray came flying towards his head, he managed to duck underneath it, hands still folded behind his back. It was apparently enough for him as he barreled through the crowd with his shoulders and rushed out of the great hall, hands folded behind his back all the way.

Zarrow was stunned to speechlessness. He knew the treatment of Eclipseborn was terrible nowadays, but he didn't realize it was *that* bad. He turned back toward Kaurazi, his hand still covering his shocked mouth.

All Kaurazi did was shrug his shoulders in a gesture that said, "I told you so." Listlessly, he picked at more of his food, chewing it thoroughly before finally swallowing. "Hence why we stay over here."

"Sorry to say it's not the first incident with Tabrum today, either," Zarrow said. When Kaurazi opened his mouth to question further, Zarrow told him of Verina's visit to the hut and, more specifically, her belief that Tabrum was responsible for her husband's death.

"Never known her to be a sane person, but still, what the hell," Kaurazi murmured. "Won't be long 'til we're blamed for the sun not comin' out at this rate."

"You're not concerned at all? About Tabrum's well-being? About your own, for that matter?"

Kaurazi threw his hands up. "What do you want me to say, Zarrow? Nothin' they say to me today is gonna be different than what they've been sayin' to me for years. Same goes for Tabrum. Same for Ceverra over there. Speakin' o' which. Hey, Ceverra."

A prolonged moment passed before Ceverra finally turned around, placing a marker in the pages of the book she had been reading. She bore a sullen expression on her face, her eyes seeming to be fighting back angry tears. She was nervously biting her lower lip, evidently a habit from the visible scabs.

"What is it?" she asked, not entirely giving either of them her full attention.

Kaurazi gestured to the empty spaces beside them. "You don't have to sit there alone. You can join us if you'd like."

Ceverra offered an acknowledging grunt but shook her head just the same. "I'm fine over here by myself, but thank you." And she turned back around.

With a shrug, Kaurazi returned to his breakfast. "Worth a try. I ask her every other day anyway," he whispered. "One o' of these days, she might say yes."

Zarrow couldn't help but chuckle despite it all.

They continued with their breakfast and casual conversation until the great hall gradually filled even more. As the flow of patrons pushed folks closer and closer to them, Zarrow and Kaurazi both agreed that it would be an excellent time to make tracks. Thankfully, their departure was much more unceremonious than Tabrum's forced exit.

Standing outside, off the beaten path and out of the way of passers-by, they discussed their plans for the remainder of the day: Kaurazi with his latest crafting project and Zarrow with his anticipated avoidance of anything to do with incense.

"All the best o' luck to you, then," Kaurazi said with a grin. "Be wonderful when all this nonsense with the dead is done and dusted. Lookin' forward to when that's all over."

"You and me both, my friend," Zarrow said. "You and me both."

They shook hands, tentatively discussing arrangements for later that evening, and then went their separate ways. Zarrow took a walk down to the shoreline, the gulls cawing overhead as his feet touched the sand. In moments of uncertainty, he always found that the ocean calmed him. The gentle crash of the waves, the slow flow of the tides. The sea always offered him a perfect avenue for reflection.

Lookin' forward to when that's all over.

Zarrow sat in the sand, grasping his hand at the Foresight pendant dangling from his neck. He grunted to himself, wondering what was in store for him were he to look ahead at what was to come.

Part of him felt as though he was playing into his father's hand of "discovering" how the shamans could commune with the dead, despite his disinterest in doing so.

"No," he assured himself. "I'm just finding out when this is all gonna be a thing of the past. That's all."

He clutched the pendant more tightly and felt a surge of light course through him. It was all a jumble of sights and sounds, an assault of the senses he was entirely unused to, even after eight years since he was granted Foresight. Images flashed before him faster than he could decipher and interpret them: scenes of the village passing by him in the span of a blink, moments of tranquility that lasted hardly a second.

But within that amalgam of possibilities, there still managed to be sensations that stood out from the rest. None of it to do with "communing with the dead." Zarrow saw none of that.

He saw fire. He heard screams. He saw a gleaming bright moon accompanied by sinister laughter. The words "curse" echoed over and over in his head.

And before he could snap out of the pendant's hold, he found himself standing before Kaurazi, both of them bloodied, hunter's knives in their hands. And then they charged one another.

The calm ocean returned to view, but Zarrow could only look down at his quivering hands in stunned silence, still feeling blood on his hands despite there being none.

His breath quickened, his heart pounded, and his mouth fell open in shock. "What the hell was that?" was all he could say.

CHAPTER TWO

The Nonsensical

The next morning, Zarrow managed to escape from home before the wave of nauseating incense awoke him. Not that sleep was going to come easy to him. How could he rest after that promise of blood and fire and curses?

And of him and Kaurazi, as well. He spent half the night staring at the ceiling, head hardly finding any comfort atop his feather-filled pillow, searching for answers as to what it all could have meant. He had never properly used his Foresight before. Was he meant to take his visions as being literal? Was there a hidden meaning within those images? He knew not the proper interpretation, and he doubted the veracity of any dreams he would have. All he could do was just...

Stare.

The night's darkness held all he could hope for at that moment as he willed his body to remain awake. Nothing but a blank slate hovering above him, an empty canvas over which the uncertainties of the future could be painted, rather than the outcome that he feared was permanently etched in stone, never to be undone or removed. He refused to peel his eyes away from that emptiness, where nothing could transpire that would confirm what he saw, confirm what he feared to lose.

Zarrow's eyes never once felt heavy within those shadows. They grew weary only when the first promises of daylight began to trickle in through the doorway, banishing his blank canvas from view and filling his world with certainty, definition. The carved clay of his ceiling, plain though it was, could have foretold the same visions deep within its cracks if Zarrow had sought his answers ardently enough.

He forced himself out of bed before such proclivities overtook him. Chancing a brief glance toward his father's incense candles, he considered but for a moment attempting to commune with the Owl, especially given Shaman Yodir had yet to wake. It had been quite some time since Zarrow had spoken with the Owl. Probably not since his Trial eight years ago. If there existed any who could help him make sense of his Foresight visions, it would have been the god who granted him the power to see them.

But that persistent fear of confirmation was all the deterrent Zarrow needed to decline, and he walked out into first light, the sky still colored a tickled pink against the morning's early glow. The ocean called for Zarrow's presence, and he was wont to refuse such a request. The seaside breeze gave him a bit of a chill against his chest, his morning robe only loosely tied. There was little point in remedying that; another hour and the air would already be sweltering. He could handle the temporary briskness of the day for the moment. He just needed to think further.

Zarrow sat himself down in the same spot as yesterday, loath to draw power from his pendant again. Instead, he only stared straight ahead at the calm waves, dancing gently by the tides' whims. The breeze fluttered his untied hair behind him, the salt air stinging his eyes as he maintained his headlong glare.

It's so beautiful here. So peaceful, he thought. *How could such horror possibly come to these shores?*

He doubted he would find his answers in the form of breaching fish and scuttling crabs, much as he would not have in the hallowed dark of his sleeping hours, but there was peace here regardless. A peace that could very well have been waning.

A soft din rose in volume in the distance as the Tribe gradually began to wake. Zarrow sighed, wondering how many more times he would be able to hear those peaceful murmurings, whether he would be able to greet those same whispering faces on his next day. If he would be fortunate enough to even *have* a next day. He slowly combed his fingers through the fine grains of sand, occasionally nicking his fingers along the edge of a seashell shard, catching one further glimpse of the ocean, shimmering in the morning light as the air, predictably, started to grow stiffer and more sweltering. He rose back to his feet, wiping sweat from his brow, eyeing a pair of crabs but finding none of the energy nor willpower necessary to procure his morning breakfast. Instead, he turned back toward the village, the great hall again looming tall.

His stomach churned, but he was not hungry. He knew he would find Kaurazi there soon enough. If there was anyone who could help him make sense of the nonsensical, it would be his dearest friend.

It was what may have soon come afterward that most turned his guts to water.

❖

Zarrow was admittedly shocked that he beat Kaurazi to the great hall. He was under the impression that his friend practically woke up in here every morning with a plate of food already in his hands.

The hall was rather quiet save for the creaking floors underfoot and the sound of a metal serving spoon scraping along the rim of a cauldron in the kitchen. Zarrow nodded in the direction of the cook, who seemed to have already been ignoring him, and plodded along toward the corner table, away from the few early risers who were less likely to return to sleep after pissing with the rising sun.

As he sat by his lonesome, Zarrow twiddled his thumbs atop the table, smacking his lips, a million and one thoughts running through his head, the ability to file them in a neat pile hardly a skill that he spent any modicum of time honing over the years. Every instinct within him wished to scream, but he instead settled for the kind of nervous twitch one was likely to display when shown a monstrous vision of kinslaying with no explanation otherwise.

He buried his face in his hands, groaning coarsely. His stomach churned once more, a cavernous pit opening inside him, sweat dripping down his forehead and pooling in his underarms, all independent of the stuffy confines of the great hall.

"Here early today, aren'cha, Zarrow?"

Zarrow could only imagine how he must have looked to Kaurazi when he removed his face from his hands, all streaky sweat and sunken eyes.

"Picture o' sunshine today, huh?" Kaurazi chuckled before seating himself across from Zarrow, letting loose a sharp whistle to request a plate of breakfast. "Went lookin' for you yesterday. Couldn't find you anywhere."

The pit in Zarrow's stomach only grew wider. "Huh?" He blinked himself back to some resemblance of attention, finally processing what Kaurazi had just said. "Ah, right. Sorry about that. I just needed some time to myself. You know, just to think."

Kaurazi absently scratched at his chin, flexing his jaw all the while. "Yeah? Any good thoughts?"

Zarrow was quick to shake his head. "No, no. Nothing like that. Just…" He trailed off, scratching at his eye. He allowed the thought to die with a short sigh. "I don't know."

"Yeah, me neither," Kaurazi said with a scoff. He inclined his brow toward Zarrow, leaning in closer with his elbow propped atop the table. "Look, Zarrow. Been through a lot together, you and me. Helped each other through so much. You got me through my parents' death fourteen years ago, treated me like a brother when I had no one else. Didn't think twice when you found out I was Eclipseborn and treated me the same as you always did. Whatever's troublin' you, don't think I'm not listenin'. I'm there for you like you for me. Promise my life on that."

Your life? Zarrow thought, forcing a smile in response. *I pray this is the one promise you don't keep.*

His eyes fixated on a pair of mice off in the corner, tumbling over one another as they attacked a scrap of food. He couldn't say for how long he focused on the sight, but it was all too entrancing. To see two creatures, perhaps even friends, fight over something so simple as crumbs.

Only when Kaurazi's breakfast plate clapped in front of him did Zarrow return to attention. He shook his head, turning back toward his friend across the table, who only quietly chomped away at some poor imitation of yesterday's meal, topped with a wad of spit rather than a heap of rice.

"Hey, talk to me," Kaurazi requested. "Otherwise, I'm gonna have to try more of the cook's new recipe here. Not quite lookin' forward to that."

Zarrow tapped his thumb against the edge of the table, glancing this way and that while the words struggled to reach his lips. The rays of light pouring in through the window started dissipating; evidently, the clouds had rolled in since he arrived at the great hall. A soft commotion began filling the vast chamber as more and more Tribespeople arrived for their morning meal. Despite the noise, despite the company across from him, Zarrow felt alone.

Despite it all, though, he managed to force a soft smile. "You ever wonder," he began, "just what's going to happen to our Tribe if it stays so obsessed with the dead? With what the dead have to say to us?"

Kaurazi shrugged as he pushed his sad plate of food away. "Figure the other Tribes will laugh at us and think we're all off our collective nut. What of it?"

"No." Zarrow shook his head. "Honestly, though. Where does it start, where does it end? *How* does it start and end? One day we're opening lines of communication with our deceased kin as though they were next-door neighbors; the next, we're, what, letting their words dictate our every move? Allowing them to subject us to their whims? Do the dead control us already? Where is that obsession going to lead us?"

"You've been spendin' too much time with your father," Kaurazi said.

"I'm serious here."

"So am I. The shamans've all lost their marbles."

"Kaurazi." Zarrow slapped his hand on the table, not loud enough for the echo to carry across the hall but still with enough volume to draw strange glances from a few tables down.

Kaurazi spread his hands in deference, inclining his head in an admission of defeat. "Okay, I'll bite. What's eatin' at you, truly? Where's all this talk of death comin' from? Not like you to get all sullen about this. Normally, you say your piece, we laugh at whatever new's come about all this nonsense, and we move on. Somethin' happened, didn't it?"

Furrowing his brow, Zarrow felt a deep frown forming, an involuntary reaction to those haunting sights still plaguing him. He tugged at the chain of his pendant, feeling the cold braided metal tug against the back of his neck. *I just had to be curious, didn't I?* he thought. *I'm only going to threaten the life of my closest friend for reasons I don't understand. I only saw our Tribe gripped in the throes of destruction due to circumstances I do not know.*

Somehow, he managed a chuckle. "Yes. Yes, I suppose you could say, 'something happened.'" He gripped the ornament of his pendant and held it up to his eyes, staring at the rune carved into its face. Such a simple rune: a horizontal line crossing the diameter of the pendant, a small tip etched to one side of the line, like an arrow shot forth, headed only in one direction with no possibility of redirection or return.

"I still haven't made sense of it all. But yesterday, I saw...visions. Fire, blood, death. And all of us party to it." The pendant shook in his hand as he recalled the more horrifying details. "I don't know when, or how, or why. I don't know whether I have any means of stopping it from happening. Is this all inevitable, preordained? Is this—"

Quickly, Kaurazi cleared his throat, raising a hand to request Zarrow to stop. "Slow down there. One thing at a time. From the beginning now. What's all this about fire and blood and death now?"

Zarrow was hoping he could breeze through the subject of the vision without any relating of the finer details, but there was no getting around it. He told Kaurazi of the chaotic scenes that played in his head, of the ear-splitting screams against a backdrop of inferno and destruction. And not a communion with the dead to be seen.

A long pause gripped them both. Kaurazi loosed a long breath, leaning back on the bench with his arms crossed. "Can't say that I'm much an expert on how Foresight works in the first place. Not a chance you can speak to your father, see if he can speak to the Owl on your behalf?"

"Are you kidding?" Zarrow barked. "He's expecting me to have been 'seeing' how we discover our communication with the dead. If I give him *this*, he's not going to hear the concerns for our Tribe. He's going to see it only as the gates to the Otherworld opening wide." He buried his face back in his hands, massaging at his tired eyes, running his fingers through his mess of locks. "All I can wonder is if it's the Owl trying to warn me. Trying to warn *us*."

Kaurazi grunted, perplexed. "Warn us? About what?"

"There was something...else. The scenery just didn't feel...natural. The moon was almost...glowing. And the night seemed to shine along with it."

"That..." Kaurazi trailed off, his brow furrowed in deep thought. "That's..."

"And in that light, there was some kind of...I don't know, laughter? And the word 'curse' over and over? It was...unsettling. Almost like it was...coming from the moon itself."

"Now you're just tryin' to fuck with me."

"I wish I was, Kaurazi. Really." Zarrow shook his head, wanting so desperately for it to be true just the same. "I don't know what I'm doing with my Foresight. I'll fully admit that. But there was one thing that was eminently clear, and it was that."

Kaurazi grimaced. "Godsdamn," he whispered.

A thought came to Zarrow, though he was hesitant to voice it. It seemed a tender line to toe, but if there was any hope of understanding Kaurazi and *his* world, then he had only to ask. It was too important not to.

"Let me ask you this," he said, hesitantly meeting Kaurazi's gaze. "Does the moon ever...*speak* to you? Or you to it? I mean, if there's any—"

Kaurazi was quick to shake his head. "Wouldn't say I've ever been on 'speaking terms' with the moon. Us Eclipseborn don't have it so scheduled as you do."

"You've never heard...anything from it?"

A flash of annoyance framed Kaurazi's face. "What do you want me to say, Zarrow?" he asked. "Can't just take a peek into the future like you can. Frankly don't even know what the moon gave to me, if anythin'. Always just been an outsider here. Nothin' to offer, nothin' to contribute. But the label still carries, and I'm still treated with the same fear and the same disregard as someone like Tabrum, who probably also never did anything for it.

"Fact is, Zarrow, I won't be surprised if that vision you saw, it has to do with us. Me and Tabrum and Ceverra and all the other Eclipseborn in the Tribe. It's always gonna be us."

Zarrow was lost for words. How was he meant to respond?

The final part of the vision, the part he dreaded relaying, lingered heavily on his mind. His head was caught in a fog, the only imagery visible the bloodied form of his dearest friend.

Is it really...inevitable? Is it really...just how it must be?

He looked pensively at Kaurazi, an anxious urge flowing through him to dig at his own flesh, chew at his nails. The silence that brewed between them was long and dense, nothing exchanged between the two friends beyond wordless nods and forced smiles. There was nothing to say; Kaurazi's words felt harsh to Zarrow, and yet...

They felt true. The Tribe was filled with people like Verina who despised the Eclipseborn for no reason other than for what they were: different. And here was Kaurazi, pouring those apprehensions out, and all Zarrow could bring himself to do was nod like a simpleton.

"Anyway," Kaurazi said, breaking the long pause. "Sorry. I...I know you didn't mean bad by the question. You're tryin' to make sense o' this. Not blamin' you at all."

"Kaurazi..." Zarrow stroked his chin, struggling to maintain eye contact with his friend. His only instinct was to slowly shake his head back and forth. "*I'm* sorry. I didn't—"

"You couldn't know." Kaurazi sighed deeply, massaging the bridge of his nose, looking down at his food once again with lingering disappointment. "Come on. Let's just get out o' here. Walk'll do us both good. Think we just need to air some o' this out, yeah?"

Zarrow nodded. "Yeah."

They both made for the doors, paying little mind to the sharp glares pointed in their direction as they departed. Zarrow was ready to leave the stagnant dry air of the great hall behind when he felt someone roughly push past him, only a barely audible apology uttered as they hurried to the corner of the hall to a secluded table.

The force of the impact turned Zarrow completely around, nearly knocking him off his feet. He eyed the person scurrying away from him, long hair tied tightly back, bouncing up and down along the base of their neck. Though their face was turned away from him, he could tell by the large book immediately dropped on the table just who it was.

He nudged Kaurazi with his elbow. "That was Ceverra, wasn't it?"

They stared at her from the entrance, jostled by the handful of people entering simultaneously, some muttering hardly-guarded obscenities in reference to them. Zarrow quickly observed Ceverra's shoulders convulsing up and down, her head in her hands, elbows propped firmly atop the table.

He furrowed his brow and, maintaining his gaze with Kaurazi, inclined his head toward Ceverra and began walking toward her. Kaurazi seemed to have no objections and followed closely behind.

As Zarrow approached Ceverra, he could hear her nose sniffling, her breath shaking. It sounded like she was holding back sobs.

Hesitantly, he tapped her on the shoulder. "Ah, Ceverra?" he said softly.

Ceverra inhaled sharply and wiped her eyes with the back of her hand. When she turned around, Zarrow was not at all surprised to see just how red and puffy her eyes were, her face still glistening wet with recent tears.

"What is it?" she asked, irritation in her voice.

Zarrow took a step back. "I...sorry." He scratched at the back of his head, his fingers getting caught in a knot of hair. "I just...wanted to check in on you. You came in here in a rush and..."

"What does that matter? A lot of people come in here in a rush."

"Not everyone immediately rushes to where no one will be sitting near them."

"Look, whatever your game here is, I don't care. I will certainly not share it with the son of a shaman. Now, please leave me alone."

Zarrow drew in a sharp breath but acquiesced. He nodded, trying to offer a gentle smile but finding only a pained glare in response. "Right, I...I'm sorry."

He turned to walk away just as Ceverra returned to her closed book, but Kaurazi walked right up to her, putting a soft hand on her shoulder. Ceverra flinched and looked ready to scream at him but stayed her voice when she seemed to realize it was not Zarrow trying it all over again.

"Sorry about him," Kaurazi said, his words quiet but just loud enough for Zarrow to hear. "He doesn't mean bad. He did just want to make sure you're okay."

"Kaurazi..." Ceverra whispered, her voice breaking once again.

"Can promise you. He's not like his father. Probably one of the few who treat Eclipseborn right in this Tribe."

Ceverra glanced at Zarrow with suspicion, apparently still unconvinced before her attention returned to Kaurazi, tears starting to well in her eyes again. "I had a...feeling. That something was going to happen. Something horrible. There's an...aura in the air."

"Your sense..." Kaurazi muttered. He looked over his shoulder toward Zarrow and quickly nodded.

Her hands shaking, Ceverra bit at her lower lip. "I told one of the shamans, and he...just laughed at me. Laughed that my aura sensing was just something I made up. And that I should...should..." She trailed off, her eyes clenching shut as her body shuddered.

Kaurazi took her hand and held it gently, clasping it with his right hand and placing his left hand on top. "Should what?" he asked.

Another sob was bit back as Ceverra breathed sharply through gritted teeth. "He said that I should...that I'd better pray to my moon that whatever is coming doesn't find its way to me." She pointed her gaze elsewhere, it apparently not being within her to glance upon either one of them anymore. "I'm frightened, Kaurazi."

She began to sob once more. Kaurazi dipped his head, still holding her quivering hands.

When Zarrow read his friend's face, all he could see was dejection, anger, and...acceptance. An acceptance that what he voiced would indeed come to pass. That Ceverra was a solemn proof of that.

He couldn't bring himself to leave, but he had no words to offer just the same. All he could manage to do was sit beside Kaurazi and helplessly listen to the soft sound of Ceverra's worried sobs.

CHAPTER THREE

The Threads of Fate

It was a long while before Zarrow could leave the great hall. Tribespeople came and went, breakfasts extended into lunches, and stuffier did the air grow amidst the mid-summer heat, but he simply could not find it in him to leave.

No words were exchanged, no communication at all beyond the subtle glances toward Kaurazi and Ceverra. Even as the hours passed, it was easier for the three of them to remain in companionable silence, tense though it was, than to voice anything in a vain attempt to ease the worries.

When the late afternoon came, Zarrow barely exchanged a cursory nod before departing. He simply patted Kaurazi on the shoulder, opting not to offer a glance toward his friend, and shuffled off to the warm salt air outside, where the sun still shone brightly, despite everything.

He wandered the village with hardly a thought, nary a destination. He couldn't even say for how long he walked. No matter the number of people who exchanged sidelong glances or admonishing words with him, Zarrow simply did not have the strength to react. Instead, the same thought ran through his mind over and over with no sign of stopping.

What can I even do?

The resignation to which Kaurazi had seemed to have submitted himself was not one that Zarrow wanted to allow for his own being. He wanted to help. He wanted desperately for what he saw to be untrue, a trick of the light. A fabrication sent to him by a deceitful god or a warning sent to him by powers he did not understand.

All of it weighed heavily on his mind as he continued his wander through the village pathways, the sea breeze calmly fluttering his waves of hair as he walked headlong into it, the world around him operating under ordinary pretenses. Conversations carried on among passersby, the smell of homemade stews wafted in the air, and the local fauna chirped and rummaged just as they always did. No one was any the wiser to what was soon to come, and that was perhaps more unsettling to Zarrow than his visions themselves.

As he observed the natural proceedings of the everyday lives play out among his Tribe, Zarrow couldn't help but wonder what even speaking of the contents of his vision would accomplish. *Is it inevitable?* he thought. *Can we do anything against it? Or is this just...fate? An inescapable, predestined fate?*

He sighed, shaking his head, his gaze drawn sullenly to the ground below, paying no heed to the foot traffic around him. The air grew louder the further he walked, an oppressive wall of noise assaulting his ears. He clenched his eyes shut, grimacing against it all. It was as though a mighty wave from the ocean was imminent to crash over him. His head pulsed with pain, throbbing in intermittent bursts against his temple. He felt a warm tinge in his Foresight pendant, a bright light blinding him.

The fires roared once again, nothing surrounding him but blood and carnage. He sweltered beneath the heat, the blazes scorching the world around him. Bodies were strewn on the ground, some contorted into unnatural positions. The sinister laughter rang in his ears again but piercing through that noise was a collective wail. Countless of his

Tribespeople wandered the streets, hands to their heads, looking this way and that, running in all directions. It was a chorus of screams. Not of pain or anguish.

But of fear.

"Get away!" one man shouted, sprinting past Zarrow, nearly passing straight through him.

"Be quiet! Shut up, shut up!" a woman bellowed, rocking back and forth in a fetal position as she clasped her hands over her ears.

Zarrow reached out, an enormous weight bearing down on his arm as he watched the hell before him. Masked individuals walked in a single file, seemingly unaffected by the chaos surrounding them. He followed their path as they trudged through the blood and blazes, each bearing a torchlight in one hand and a small blade in the other. They fanned out, all in the direction of the discarded, lifeless bodies strewn about the village.

The face of the body closest to him was turned away as a masked individual knelt beside it. The person's voice was soft but still managed to carry over the rippling flames.

"May the blood of the cursed be expunged from our people and cleansed in your hands. I return this body to you so their voice may return to me." And they drove the knife into the dead body's abdomen, cutting a deep crimson swath, the blood coursing out of the gash in a flowing river. As the blood flowed, the masked individual reached both hands into the opening and *pulled*, the sound absolutely sickening to Zarrow's ears. The body was turned over onto its stomach, the earth underneath soaking in blackened red. It was only when the body was turned that Zarrow was able to see the face.

"Kaurazi."

Zarrow tried in desperation to run toward his friend, but his body would not cooperate. He could do nothing but watch. A wave of nausea rose within him, his body numb as he watched the masked individual raise their hands to the skies over Kaurazi's eviscerated body in silence, almost as though in prayer.

When Zarrow at last vomited, the flames disappeared, the stench of death vanished, and disgusted groans murmured beside him.

"Ugh, nasty," he heard a voice say.

As he opened his eyes again, Zarrow found the village back at its normal paces, passersby flashing him annoyed and repulsed glances as he knelt on all fours in the middle of the pathway, the acrid taste of bile lingering on his tongue and in the back of his throat. A tremor roared through him, a weakness overtaking his arms and legs. His lungs felt heavy, his breathing labored.

"Oh gods, oh gods," he whispered to the ground and his vomit upon it.

"Out of the way, you drunk," another passerby said, barreling him out of the way with a knee to the shoulder, knocking Zarrow off-balance, narrowly avoiding landing in his own sick.

Zarrow felt frozen. Despite the dirt being kicked up and the spittle raining down on him, he couldn't move. He couldn't break from that horrid imagery. He couldn't fathom the bloodlust.

All that broke him from his trance was a shrill shriek from up the main drag.

"You godsdamned murdering *bastard!*"

His head a groggy mess, Zarrow wearily rose to his feet. A rush of curious onlookers pushed past him, disregarding the pile of vomit, all called by the source of the noise. Zarrow followed them, though not at the same furious pace, clasping a hand to his temple in an attempt to quell the throbbing aches still rumbling in his skull.

The crowd gathered at the path's mouth, where the village opened to a central square upon which all paths converged. Zarrow shoved his way to the outskirts of the crowd, ignoring a handful of protests in so doing, and settled at the end of the line, still able to have a clear view of the proceedings.

In the square stood two people, a woman and an older man, spread several feet apart from one another. They regarded one another in cold, tense silence, the man keeping his hands folded behind his back while the woman maintained an accusatory finger toward him. As Zarrow squinted his eyes, he finally realized that the two were none other than Verina and Tabrum.

"Oh no," Zarrow muttered under his breath. He had no inkling as to how much longer Verina had lingered with his father yesterday, but it was clear she had still remained adamant in her previous assertions regarding her deceased husband.

"Do you still deny it, then?" Verina shouted, her voice carrying as though she were right beside Zarrow.

Tabrum shrugged his shoulders, his body language all weariness, the lifetime of mistreatment seeming to weigh an immense amount upon him. Zarrow had only ever known him as a belligerent old man—though he could never blame him for it—but in this moment, Tabrum simply appeared...tired. Missing entirely that angry fire that always burned within him.

"I no longer know what you want me to tell you, Verina," he said, the wind carrying his voice along to Zarrow.

"Only the truth!" Verina yelled, waving her arms to her side. "The truth that you killed my dearest Sepet in cold blood!"

Tabrum shook his head, his shoulder sagging. "I have given you the truth. It is simply not the truth that you want to hear, the truth that you have invented for yourself."

"Then I am *sure* you would love to inform me of the 'truth' of your whereabouts the night my Sepet was killed!"

"I have told you, and I am sure many others have as well: Sepet passed in his sleep. There is nothing malicious in that."

"You avoid the question because you have nothing to prove your innocence!" Verina turned in place, extending her arms to the surrounding crowd as though soaking in an assured victory. She displayed a wide grin on her face, one that Zarrow found absolutely sickening.

Tabrum slowly put his hands on his hips, again shaking his head. "I was at my home. Far from yours. Alone, as I always am."

Zarrow winced at those final words. His thoughts returned to Kaurazi and Ceverra sitting together in an accepting, sullen silence. Despite the friendship that Zarrow shared with Kaurazi his entire life...was his friend always alone, as well?

Verina began to chuckle, that grin of hers growing even more revolting. "And, so, there is none who can prove you to have nothing to do with my husband's murder."

"And, likewise," Tabrum retorted, "there is none who can prove that I had *anything* to do with your husband's *death*." He placed extra emphasis on the final word, as though to drive home the point that Sepet was not murdered.

"It matters not at all," Verina said, amusement in her tone. "The proof shall be there. We need only wait."

"You will be waiting until the end of your days, Verina. What cause would I have had to kill your husband, to begin with?"

Verina sneered and scoffed, appearing to take great offense to the query. "You would ask *that*, as though you do not already know? What more cause do you need than being what you are?" She took three giant steps toward Tabrum, closing the gap between them. "You are nothing more than an ill-bred *Curseborn*! Your *kind* stands counter to everything we are as a people. What greater cause do you have as a...a...an *agent of despair*! That you have wallowed so long in your own misery that you must ensure that the rest of us suffer that same fate!"

A flash of anger shone upon Tabrum's face. "What are these words? 'Curseborn?' 'Agent of despair?' Are you even listening to yourself? Do you hear the absurdity of your words?"

The gap closed even more until Verina and Tabrum could nearly touch noses. "There is no absurdity in my words but for the fact that they should be more pointed than they already are. But *you*—" She jabbed a finger into his chest.

"Please do not do that, Verina. Please." It almost seemed as though there was panic in Tabrum's eyes.

"I shall do what I please, you bastard. Just as *you* did as *you* pleased that night." She reached behind her back, finding the grip of her hunter's knife sheathed at her waist.

"Verina…" Tabrum's voice had an undertone of warning to it. "I will only ask you once more…"

"Did my husband beg in the same way as you? Did you *revel* in it?"

"I reveled in nothing because I did not—"

"Because *I* shall—"

"—kill your—"

"—revel in—"

"—husband!"

"—*this!*"

"No!"

Verina quickly drew her blade, the scrape of steel echoing along with the voice of the wind. Zarrow and several others rushed forward in some attempt to reach the pair before it reached a point of no return. As Zarrow sprinted ahead, he caught the sense of resignation in Tabrum's eyes.

The old man held his hands out, planting them against Verina's shoulders as though to keep her at arm's length. Tabrum closed his eyes, drawing a long breath.

Zarrow did not know if his eyes deceived him or if he did truly see a tear stream down the elder's cheek.

The knife was barely out of its sheath when Verina suddenly dropped to the ground, all the strength leaving her body at once, the momentum of the blade causing it to slide away off to the side.

Everyone stopped in their tracks in confusion. Tabrum looked down at his hands, his old, shaking hands. In his eyes was a waning flame comprised of what appeared to be anger, regret, sadness...and perhaps even resignation. He looked at the gathered crowd, another tear falling, and he closed his eyes again with another deep breath.

One of the Tribesmen beside Zarrow, a tall man wearing simple robes and fashioning his hair in a tight bun, cautiously approached Verina's body, holding his hands out to Tabrum as though to indicate he meant no harm. He knelt beside Verina, putting two fingers to her throat, looking for a pulse, before he drew his hand away.

Fear flashed upon his face as he turned back toward Zarrow and the rest of the crowd. "She's dead," he said softly.

Nobody seemed to comprehend his words at first. Zarrow looked from one person to another, disbelief strewn upon each of their faces, some shaking from the shock, others staring at Tabrum with mouths agape, pointing accusatory fingers at the old man.

The silence at last broke when someone shouted, "M-murderer!"

"He killed her!"

"Someone, get the shamans!"

"Murderer!"

"*Murderer!*"

The crowd dispersed, save for Zarrow, who kept his eyes on Tabrum. Shrieks and proclamations filled the air as the village came alive around the dead, but Zarrow was the only one who stayed put, no one else daring to remain in the presence of the Eclipseborn.

"Tabrum..." Zarrow whispered, his voice only barely carrying.

The old man spared a final glance for the departed Verina. "I warned her," he said, not quite directing his words toward Zarrow, even though Zarrow was the only one remaining from the crowd. He looked back down at his trembling hands, clenching them into fists. "I did not ask for any of this." He shook his head and slowly ambled to Verina's discard blade. "Curse the moon that cursed me with this."

He knelt and picked up the blade, turning back toward Zarrow. He had an accepting smile on his face, soft and kind, betraying every perception Zarrow previously had of him. *This* was the true Tabrum, before the world battered him into what he was.

With a final quick breath, Tabrum whispered, "Forgive me."

And then he slashed the blade across his own throat.

Blood erupted from the gash as the old man collapsed in a heap. No final pleading twitches, no requests for a reprieve. Just a solemn acceptance of what had happened and a resignation for what had to be.

Zarrow felt numb, dumbfounded. He looked down at his pendant, grasping it with his trembling hand, and his breath caught in his throat. In a blink, the blazes and screams returned, only for the flames to disappear by the next.

But the screams still remained. The cries for retribution, the calls for the shamans to remedy a blight overtaking the Tribe.

And as the sun began to disappear over the western horizon, the moon started to glow in a pale light in the late afternoon sky.

All Zarrow could feel in his heart was an overwhelming sense of dread. He could only imagine where he was woven within these threads of fate.

CHAPTER FOUR

THE PALE NIGHT

Hell had already begun to break loose by the time Zarrow returned home. Bellows for retribution and justice were ringing in the early dusk air as a crowd began congregating outside the hut. Indistinct voices melded together, all manners of protest overlapping in a cacophony of anger, fear, and anguish. Just to get inside required Zarrow to nearly knock several people off their feet. The battering he suffered to his head and arms as he shoved his way through was merely a consequence he would have to ignore.

Inside the hut only dwelt further chaos. All the village's shamans—a council of twelve—had assembled, their words an inane jumble behind their ceremonial masks, muffled just enough not to make sense over the persistent and surrounding noise. Some of the Tribespeople had managed to squeeze their way into the small confines of the hut, the central chamber near to capacity as Zarrow shouldered his way past the gathering.

If there was any mercy, it was that the sheer volume of people inside had diluted the rich smell of incense enough for it to be palatable to Zarrow's nose and stomach.

He spotted his father off in the corner, hunched over the table, his mask lifted atop his head as he rummaged through the notes piled high, indecipherable scribblings coating each sheet in a strange canvas of diagrams, shapes, and something resembling substitutes for words. As the discussions continued to permeate the room in a pervasive din, Zarrow stepped around Tribespeople and shamans alike, brusquely grasping his father's forearm as he finally reached him.

"Father!" he shouted, his voice only barely carrying over the din. "What's going on? This is madness!"

Yodir knocked Zarrow's hand away, muttering something to himself as his eyes trailed along the crisscrossing paths of his notes. He tutted his lips and flashed a sly grin toward his son, something akin to malice glowing in his eyes. "You and I have gravely different understandings of the word 'madness,' Zarrow."

Zarrow quickly gestured to the crowd, spreading his right arm wide. "This! What you see before you is madness! We have to stop before—"

"Stop?" Yodir chuckled to himself, shaking his head. He held his hands out to the notes, taking in the findings almost lustfully. "Why would I stop? Why should any of us stop? I look at *this* before me—" He gestured to the piles of paper, the meaning behind it all still wholly lost on Zarrow. "—and see only discovery. The time is upon us, Zarrow." He clasped a firm hand behind Zarrow's head, pulling his son closer. "Our prayers have at last been answered."

Despite his attempts to bob and weave out of his father's grip, Zarrow stayed put, forced to glance at the madness in Yodir's eyes. "You don't mean..."

"Just so." Yodir's teeth flashed against the candlelight, their size intimidating as though a wolf had approached Zarrow and declared him to be prey. "The Owl has answered us. Everything we have searched for, everything we have sought..." He slapped a firm hand onto the piles of paper, sending sheets flying in every direction. "The path to our communion with the Otherworld is opened!"

Amusement and satisfaction upon his face, Yodir turned over his shoulder, taking in the assembled crowd. "Look at them all. Passion and pride within each of them. All wishing for the same, joining us for a common cause. Listen to them!"

Zarrow grabbed his father by the collar and pulled him in closer. "Listen to *yourself*! There's no 'common cause' here, Father! These people aren't begging to speak with the dead; they're simply frightened! Some of them were just witnesses to a murder! The Tribe is in a panic!"

The amusement and malice did not disappear from his father's face. If anything, the combination only grew more intense. "Yes, and by the hands of an Eclipseborn, was it not?"

Zarrow's eyes widened as he stammered. "I...I..."

"Was. It. Not?" Yodir repeated, the amusement disappearing, leaving the malice to take free reign.

With hesitation, Zarrow nodded.

Yodir's lips creased into a smile, something which would have passed for sympathy under ordinary circumstances. "It is but a shame that it had to be Verina. We have always known the Eclipseborn to be unnatural to our way of life, but I had no illusions that they would be so bold as to strike in broad daylight. It is a tragedy, but one that shall not go unavenged. You mustn't fear that, Zarrow."

Zarrow backed away, bumping shoulders with one of the nearby Tribsepeople. Ice ran down his spine and through his veins, his body convulsing ever so slightly. Fear was being thrown about so broadly. What his father interpreted as "fear" was nothing more than a lack of understanding.

The Eclipseborn are not "unnatural," Zarrow thought. *They are just different from us.*

Clenching his fists, Zarrow felt flashes of the true source of his fear: the memories of his visions. The clear and the unclear. The flashes of pain and rage intermingled with the vivid imagery of blood, ravaging, and destruction. The idea that he was party to it, and the feeling that its fulfillment was drawing ever so near, so close that he could already feel the spatter of blood coating his hands. Once again, and for the first time.

Yodir took note of Zarrow's trembling form and drew closer to his son, extending a hand that was not received. "My son," he said, a false warmth coating his words. "Quiver no longer. The time is at hand. Verina will be a martyr under whom we shall champion this night, for whom we will raise a banner to the depths of the Otherworld."

Zarrow held both hands out, the promise of the night sending a further chill coursing through him. "Father...do not do this." The laughter echoed in his head once more, the moon's pale glow freezing everything within him.

His father moved past him toward the center of the room, patting a firm hand atop Zarrow's shoulder. "I do only as our gods wish and instruct. This shall ever be our way."

The crowd encircled Yodir as though he were a prophet. Zarrow tried to push his way through, but they enclosed themselves so quickly that all he accomplished was being thrown from one side to the other. He saw his father raise his hands up high as he always did when deep in prayer before the incense candles, but this felt like something more. Something...

Vile.

Zarrow felt his robe entangle within the fold of someone's arm, the sharp tug preventing him from making his way through to the front of the crowd to quell his father's madness. As he futilely attempted to pry free the threads of his robe from an inattentive attendee, the pervasive din of the assembly finally quieted.

"My dearest friends," Yodir began, a friendly tone to his voice. "I have heard your fears this evening. I, too, share in them, I assure you.

A shadow has been cast over our Tribe for far too long, and we are long overdue to shine a light over it, to cast this foul darkness from our midst. Left unchecked, the horror that shook us this evening will spread. As we would a weed, we must pluck it before it takes root.

"It is what we must do. It is what the gods wish for us to do. They have heard our pleas, the pleas of we shamans, to reach to the plane of those we have lost, to hear their words, listen to their wisdom. From that plane, we shall have light once more, glowing brilliantly upon the Dusk Tribe from this day until our final days, a radiance that shall no longer permit the shadows to come near us again."

The crowd listened intently to Yodir's every word as Zarrow finally pried himself loose from the uncaring bystander. He was three rows of people back from his father, two rows, one. A wall of shamans stood at the front of the crowd, filed in behind Yodir in a subservient line, heeding his sermon, nodding along as they took in the speech.

Yodir turned to the shamans, seeming to pay no attention to his own son trying to fight his way through to the front. He held a hand out towards them, his fingers bent inwards like vicious talons.

"My friends, my brothers," he said, his gaze focused squarely upon the shamans. "Our time of enlightenment is at hand. No longer will we live in fear of a dark age ruled by the shadows in our midst. Round up the Eclipseborn." He paused, narrowing his eyes as he took a deep breath before lowering his mask back down. "And eliminate them."

Behind the mask, the words seemed to echo. They reverberated across the room, passing from one person to the next, each relaying the order with mixtures of surprise, elation, and shock. The raucous din returned, immediate discussions overlapping one another.

Do they even realize what is being said? Zarrow wondered. *Do they even know what he's talking about, to begin with?*

Regardless of the obscene order, no one was in any rush to carry out the deed. The shamans stood at attention, a hunter's knife resting at each of their waists, but they did not grab for them. They did not brandish them to hoist into the air, to turn loose a rallying cry. They just stood. And waited. Perhaps soaking in the moment. It certainly appeared that Yodir was doing so, with arms outstretched, turning in place to face all who stayed to hear his words.

I don't want to imagine what kind of horrid expression is hidden behind that mask.

The only person in the crowd who had made any effort to move was Zarrow himself. He finally shoved his way past the gawkers and onlookers, avoiding the host of shamans entirely as he approached his father. From all the rattling and pushing within the crowd, Zarrow's robe had come untied, exposing much of his chest, his Foresight pendant bouncing rhythmically, and his hair was loose and unkempt in front of his face. He had to imagine he bore the image of a vagrant.

"I told you this was madness," Zarrow said sharply through gritted teeth to his father, brushing a tuft of hair out of his face with his hand. "We cannot allow this to happen, Father. You all—" He pointed to the other shamans. "—cannot possibly wish to go along with this. You are talking about murdering innocent people. Members of our Tribe!"

"It is not murder," Yodir said from behind his mask, his voice muffled and deepened from the dense composition of the wood. "But sacrifice. A betterment for our people."

"It is *genocide*, Father! Do *not* try to coat your words in such lies."

Some of the assembly had begun to take notice of Zarrow's exchange with his father. The commotion quelled ever so softly.

Yodir puffed his chest, broadened his shoulders, and stepped toward his son. He gave Zarrow a painful prod to the chest with his finger. "Do *not* presume to lecture me, Zarrow. We are doing only as the gods have willed us. And if—"

"Does that make it *right*?" Zarrow interrupted, closing the gap between him and his father. "Or are you merely looking for an excuse?

To slaughter our own people in chase of some...macabre fantasy that you have? Because if the gods willed us to kill our own—"

"They are not our own, Zarrow!" Yodir was near to bellowing. "They are abnormalities, wicked creatures spawned by a devil! If the gods wish them to be cast from their sight, then it is our duty to do so!"

"And just what *did* the gods say to you, Father?" The volume of their argument reached a higher decibel, the assembled crowd now focused entirely on the loud discussion. "What words did they utter to you that sanctioned murder? What wisdom did the Owl impart upon you that doing so would allow us to commune with the Otherworld?"

Yodir waved a dismissive hand and turned his back to Zarrow. "That is not for you to know," he said with a scoff. "It is only via we dedicated faithful that the words of the Bear, the Wolf, and the Owl are given flesh. Likewise, such commands may only be interpreted by—"

"Stop, just stop!" Zarrow was near to pulling his hair out by the roots. He shuffled in place, his hands clenching at either side of his temple, his teeth gritting. "For what reason would the gods allow this if they knew it would merely bring us to our inevitable ruin?"

His father lifted his mask, his raised brow signaling amusement at the words. "Ruin?" he chuckled. "My boy, we are but steps away from—"

"Ruin!" Zarrow repeated, loud enough for all to hear. He gripped tightly to his Foresight pendant and tugged it forward, flashing it in his father's face. "Would the Owl truly wish for such slaughter if It knew the devastation that would fall upon our Tribe as a result? Or are you simply hiding behind false words to justify your own ends?"

The amusement vanished from Yodir's face. Stern did his expression grow, his arms crossed, his eyes firing arrows into his son's chest. "So you *did* see something. At last." A wide grin stretched his face, his teeth glistening like a dog licking its chops before a fresh meal. "Did you see the answer? Did we do it?"

Zarrow's jaw dropped, his mind assaulted by a flurry of disbelief. For those first few moments, it was all he could do to stop and stare at his father in silence, watch that ravenous glare in those fiery eyes. "You hardly care at all, don't you?" he said, the words only barely carrying past his tongue. "You've blinded yourself. You would watch our people burn just to see if the ashes speak to you."

"And if the ashes *do* speak, then I have done my duty."

The words hung in the air, dense and heavy. Each of those present watched the exchange with bated breath, the tension rich throughout the room.

"And if our people are thereby cursed in so doing," Zarrow spoke softly, nearly a whisper, "would you still stand proud atop those ashes?"

Yodir stared in a prolonged silence for one blink, two blinks, three. And then he tilted his head back in uproarious laughter, beckoning with his hands for others to join in, a sparse contingent joining, if only in a nervous and apprehensive manner.

"You speak of *curses*, my son?" the shaman said, wiping away a handful of tears as his chuckles subsided. "Did you have a nightmare and mistake it for truth? Shall I remain at your bedside all throughout this night?" A further collection of laughter erupted from the crowd.

Zarrow tensed his fists, drawing a deep breath through his nose. "I know what I saw, Father!" he asserted, pointing an accusatory finger. "And I know what I heard. If we walk down this road, the consequences will be only severe for us all. We *will* be cursed—by what or whom, I do not know—but the burden will be upon *you* should such befall us!"

Yodir planted his hands on his hips and shook his head, disappointment settling into his furrowed brow. As wisps of incense danced about the hut, passing from person to person, Yodir eyed his son with what appeared to be suspicion. Anger. Perhaps regret?

"I thought I raised you to be a wiser man, Zarrow," he murmured, his voice like ice. "The Owl's Boon is wasted upon one such as you."

Raising his head high, Zarrow turned his nose down at his father and gritted his teeth again. "As it is upon you, as well. You are no paragon of the Owl's wisdom. You are just a fearmonger, using this night's tragedy to further your own goals with hardly a care for the consequences. You would doom us all simply to satisfy your own ego."

The assembly remained whisper-quiet, nothing save the squeaking of mice making so much as a peep. Rows upon rows of eyes remained frozen in attention, bodies still as carved statues. The faces blended together, all bearing the same fearful and concerned glances.

All except for Yodir. If looks could kill, Zarrow's father would be the greatest murderer of all. After this night, he may still yet be.

"Entirely ludicrous," he muttered.

Zarrow raised his brow at the remark. "Ludicrous?"

Yodir turned and looked toward the entryway, the last rays of sunlight disappearing from view, so far as Zarrow could tell with the slim vestige of the outside world he could still see. A rumble echoed in his father's throat, something bordering on a groan. "It is that friend of yours, is it not? The Eclipseborn."

He has a name, Zarrow thought. *And you are not half the man Kaurazi is.* He growled at the obtuse mention, his hands balling into fists, his nails digging into his palms, near to draw blood from the force. "What of him?" he responded.

Peering off into the distance, his eyes closed in what appeared to be pensive thought, Yodir looked almost forlorn. "The foul, blasphemous words you speak could only be those of an Eclipseborn." He turned back to face Zarrow. "You would accuse your father of misleading our Tribe, and yet, here you are, spewing tall tales in a meager attempt to protect your illborn friend, one who was rejected by the gods for his vile birth."

"Father, the only vile one among us is *you!*" Zarrow shot forward, grabbing his father by the collar.

Yodir was undeterred. "If we are to be cursed, then we have been cursed already with his presence and that of his other filthy kin. Elsewise, the idea a curse shall befall us is ludicrous."

Zarrow sneered, still holding tight to his father's shamanic robe, his nails cutting swaths into the thin threads. "The only thing that is ludicrous is the idea that we can commune with the dead, and sacrificing members of our Tribe will do nothing towards that beyond demonizing you in the eyes of history."

"Well, then." Yodir chuckled deeply and pulled his mask down, the carved wood bearing more and more resemblance to the monster hiding behind it. "If history shall chronicle this night, then let me invite you to join the lost numbers."

And he struck his son, a mighty fist to the nose, nearly knocking Zarrow off his feet.

Bright spots clouded Zarrow's vision, his eyes watering, his nose throbbing, a slick streak beginning to stream down the bridge of his nose. The air seemed to grow thin as the assembly collectively gasped at the sight, unsure what to do, uncertain how to react.

As his nose pulsed with spilled blood, Zarrow put his two forefingers to his bridge, the tips coming away dark red. He snarled through the pain, winced away a grimace.

And with a bellow, he charged his father, knocking him to the ground, landing two quick jabs to the mask, his knuckles coming away with splinters as a fracture formed in the frame.

Growling, Yodir shoved his son off of him, Zarrow falling onto his back, his head hitting hard against the stone floor as another swirling daze laid claim to his vision. The world spun, but he could still see his father rise back to his feet, hear a shrill scrape as a blade was drawn clear of its sheath.

And distant yet near, his father's voice rang loud and clear:

"Find the Eclipseborn and kill them all in the name of your gods!"

There was the briefest of pauses, as though the world froze into a singular empty moment, the final thread of fate being woven through the loom until it finally erupted back into motion. An explosion of movement overtook the chamber, Zarrow returning to his feet just in time to feel a horde of people crash into him, a kiss of steel filling the space he had just occupied.

He only hazarded a scarce glance at the group he assumed to be his saviors before they scurried back off somewhere into the chaos. The stars in his eyes had finally disappeared, his vision slowly returning, and Zarrow could survey the room once again.

At one end, a rush of people made for the doorway, a bottleneck forming as people screamed in pain, screamed in anger, screamed in fright. Amidst calls to gather the Eclipseborn also dwelt pleas simply to be permitted to leave. A few of the shamans only exacerbated the situation, shoving sharply from behind, the crowd crush only worsening, cracks forming in the stone and clay tableau of the doorframe as dust started to kick up in greater fury.

Closer to him, Zarrow observed two sides forming against one another: one rushing to his own support, rallying around him; the other filing in amongst the shamans, Zarrow's father leading the charge on that front. The remaining shamans all had blades drawn and masks down, a faceless entourage threatening death under the guise of the pursuit of knowledge.

Zarrow's head still swirled as he observed the flurry of action before him. Numerous villagers, countless of his kin and compatriots, rushed the bladed shamans wielding nothing but their own fists, damning the danger, disregarding the inevitability of their own demise, focusing only on stopping the nightmare that Zarrow had promised.

"We will not allow this nightmare to pass!" shouted one of his supporters just as a blade was driven between his ribs. Despite the strike, the man managed to drive two hard headbutts into the mask of the shaman before him, fracturing it in half before taking another blade to the chest.

"For the future of our Tribe!" Zarrow heard another person cry out as they led a rush toward the wall of people standing in front of him.

So distracted was Zarrow that he hadn't recognized that he had pinned himself against the wall, flanked on one side by the still-lit incense candles and the other by his father's table of notes. Some twenty or thirty supporters barricaded him from the attackers, arming themselves with whatever nearby implements they could grab: stones, pens, inkwells, even their shoes. All in defense of Zarrow.

All in defense of the truth and the nightmare to prevent.

The shamans were undeterred, their followers much the same. As Zarrow's supporters charged ahead, they fell one by one to flashes of steel, knocked off balance by blows to the head, still maintaining a bravery in the face of oblivion that Zarrow had never before seen in his people. There was a resilience in them, fully willing to take on a murderous hand before their own lives were grasped by that hand. Even with makeshift weapons, they held their ground, striving to find openings to jab with pens, smashing inkwells atop opponents' heads, trying desperately to pry blades away from adept hands.

Some succeeded in the attempt. Just as soon as steel tasted flesh did it change hands, a couple combatants permitting the blade to score their flesh before dragging their assailant within their guard, disarming them, and then dis-arming them. But even as his protectors had gained for themselves proper weaponry, Zarrow knew it was only a fleeting opportunity. For each who stood their ground, two more fell to the hands of the better-skilled. The wall before him was crumbling.

As was the doorway, where the crowd crush had only worsened. Shamans were quite literally cutting a swath through the crowd as panicked cries rang into the air to hurry through the passageway. The doorframe continued to exhibit cracks and chips, dusty pebbles trickling down to the ground, powder puffing into the faces of those only attempting to leave.

Zarrow's first instinct was to rush toward them, help in whatever meager way he could. But the thought of only worsening the situation deterred him.

Just as much as a blade whirling toward his head did.

He ducked under the steel's arc just in time, rolling to the side, bumping into the rear guard of his protective wall. Looking up, he saw the cracked mask of his father staring back at him, the wood caked in blood and viscera as though it were part of the horror tales he was told as a child. Yodir's chest rose and fell, his breath wheezing behind the mask. The threads of his robe wore torn, the flesh of his left shoulder exposed where something had managed to slice through. His previously pristine appearance had been painted in a messy red, a canvas of his own design, with contributions from other collaborators in the room.

Zarrow opened his mouth to plead with his father, but Yodir screamed and charged forward before he could even do so. Zarrow rolled to the side, the steel echoing on the hard stone floor. A successive swing missed Zarrow by a hair, scraping instead against the adjacent wall. Seeing his opportunity, Zarrow pushed himself to his feet and tackled his father by the waist, throwing him to the ground with enough force to dislodge the blade from his hand.

The two men wrestled each other on the ground, Yodir holding back Zarrow's arms by the strength of his own. Zarrow's muscles already began to ache; he was not suited for violence such as this. Before he had time to protest, he felt a knee take him in the stomach, clearing the wind entirely out of him. He bounced onto the floor, hacking up a lung, when he felt his father's presence looming over him again. He heard the scrape of steel as it was picked up off the floor. He was dragged up to his knees by the robe collar, his ribs and lungs still suing for peace.

When he at last looked up to face his death, a swirl of motion flashed past him. Two combatants collided with Yodir, knocking the shaman clean into the wall, his blade falling to who-knows-where. Zarrow heard his father grunt in pain as the two interrupters landed blow after blow to Yodir's ribs and face, the mask cracking more and more under each fist.

When it finally splintered into pieces, a deep gash broke Yodir's skin from brow to lip, wooden shards clinging to his face like quills, redirecting the blood which streamed down his chin and throat.

As voices and steel continued to scream throughout the room, Zarrow pushed himself back up to his shaky legs, bellowed something resembling a war cry, and rushed forth, throwing his arms wide and catching his father at his broad shoulders. Yodir aimed a headbutt but missed, instead finding the brunt of Zarrow's chest with the top of his head. Zarrow wheezed as though the failed headbutt landed like a brutal punch. He was confident a bone or two had cracked within him. But, with his momentum, he was still able to slam Yodir's back straight into the wall, a pained gasp a reward to his ears.

His two supporters resumed their assault on Yodir when a warm splash coated the side of Zarrow's face. From the corner of his eye, he could see the tip of a blade sticking out through the neck of the man to his right. Before he could blink, the blade had swung forward, taking with it the rest of the man's throat, sending blood gushing forth like a waterfall.

A tall shaman bore down on Zarrow and his surviving ally, his steel still glistening with thick blood. The blade danced around them, spraying life matter every which way like an over-readied paintbrush, the left arm removed from his ally, Zarrow moving in step with the swings, a deadly waltz of their own making. The opposing shaman yelled in frustration at his continued misses, screaming for Zarrow to stay still. Zarrow saw no reason to do so.

Just as he wove in and out of the direction of another flurry of strikes, Zarrow felt a tug beneath both his arms, and suddenly his feet were dragged out from under him. He squirmed in his father's tight clutches, pulling his body to the right and to the left, but Yodir held firmly, positioning his son to face a judgment of steel in this baptism of fire.

"Now!" he heard Yodir scream, voice raspy.

Zarrow continued to pry at his father's hands, throwing his shoulders back in a futile effort. He was tired. So very, very tired.

As the shaman raised the blade for a forward thrust, Zarrow's incapacitated ally jumped forth, even with an arm missing, wailing through the agony, biting at the shaman's sword hand, blood pouring out from his teeth.

It gave Zarrow all the opportunity he needed. *If I can't break free,* he thought, looking down at his feet, *then just go down with me!*

He kicked his foot back, wrapping it around the back of his father's ankle, and pushed forward. He felt the balance tipping, his father standing only on one leg. It was time.

Zarrow pushed backward with all his might, falling into his father's body. Yodir could not handle his son's weight on one leg. Zarrow's stomach churned as he felt himself dropping, Yodir's hands still clasped about his chest. There was a sickening bump on the way down, a thunderous crack, the sky suddenly raining paper upon him. Faintly, he could hear a smattering of gasps.

There was a sharp pain in the back of his neck. His hand came away red when he touched his fingers to it, feeling a tender area where wooden shards were jutting out. His father's grasp had slackened, and though his head was in an immediate fog, Zarrow still pushed himself to his feet as quickly as he could manage.

When he looked down, he saw a splash of blood coating his father's table, his notes now written in that same shade of red. A crimson pulp pooled on the corner of the table, chips of bone sitting in the puddle. As his eyes continued their path, he noticed his father's eyes frozen open in suspended shock. He knelt down, something wet soaking through his trousers. Even in this shadowed corner, Zarrow could tell it was blood. All puddling out from behind his father's head. Zarrow turned Yodir over and found a hole where the back of his skull was meant to be.

There would be no ashes for his father to stand upon. He was gone.

Against the backdrop of crumbling stone and panicked cries, Zarrow could only numbly stare down at the man who was once his father. Whoever he was now, Zarrow did not recognize. Not anymore.

The shaman nearest to him fought off his armless attacker, knocking him off balance and driving the blood-slickened blade through the man's throat. Dust and pebbles rained down from above, creating a dense and grainy mist within the room. Zarrow turned his head toward the shaman who withdrew the blade, the teeth marks upon his wrist dripping blood.

The fractures were spreading in the wall behind him. The screams reached their zenith, the bodies of those felled by the shamans' blades piling up. The smell of acrid smoke wafted through the cracks, burning at Zarrow's nostrils. He allowed the nearby shaman to approach him, to thrust his steel towards him.

He evaded the blow, tucking the steel between his arm and his ribs, grabbed onto the shirtsleeves of his attacker, and *swung* him into the wall.

Through the wall.

The ceiling was wavering overhead. The pebbles became stones, and the stones became dangerous. His vision was obscured by the dust clouds rising from the ground, his ears filled with the cacophony of echoing crashes and fearful shrieks pleading for safety and rescuing. As the walls collapsed around him, Zarrow turned for the hole he had just created and dove, landing face-first in the outside dirt, rolling further from the hut as it fell in on itself. As he chanced a final glance inside, at the place that had been his home for his entire life, he saw a rain of papers marred by madness stained in ink and blood before the remaining ceiling crashed to the floor, covering everyone and everything that remained inside.

Including the husk of the man who had once been his father.

Zarrow propped himself up on all fours, the clay dust assaulting his lungs. He was caked in it, his skin stained white, almost as though he were a ghost. A ghost that his father was so eager to commune with.

He stumbled to his feet, his gait unsteady, a furious pain hammering away at his skull. The screams so near felt immediately distant, the calls for help beneath that rubble, the victims of a man's monstrous calls for glory. He couldn't help them. There was no saving them, not on his own. But there was one person he *could* save. One person he *needed* to save.

And his home was burning.

His left leg scored with pain, Zarrow began to shuffle down toward Kaurazi's hut, his lungs protesting with every panicked breath he took. After a handful of steps, he felt something clutching his ankle, and he instinctively kicked it away, meeting something hard upon impact, feeling a enormous crack as he did so. A howl of agony coursed through his leg.

When he looked down, he saw the shaman he had thrown through the wall. He seemed somewhat mangled, his body covered in blood and dust, one of his arms bent at an angle it should not have been.

Half of his mask had broken off, likely from the impact of the broken wall, and the other half had splintered under the weight of Zarrow's foot.

He looked like he wanted to say something with those mangled lips, but Zarrow had neither the time nor the inclination to listen. Zarrow aimed another kick at the exposed half of the shaman's face and walked on.

The flames had engulfed the interior of Kaurazi's home by the time Zarrow reached it. He tried entering it, but the heat was already far too oppressive to even attempt it.

"Kaurazi!" he shouted at the top of his lungs, his chest straining with the effort. Tears welled in his eyes as he pushed through the pain. He circled the hut, managing nothing more than a limp-run as agony continued to shoot up the length of his leg. "Kaurazi, godsdamn it, where are you?"

Distant screams pierced the night air once again, separate from those at his former home. Pyres grew tall along the southern horizon, scorching the roofs of huts like bonfires. He could barely make out the shadowed visages of two bodies chasing a third, tackling the form to the ground. As arms were raised in what was either protest or a reprieve, a set of fists fell like a hammer, smashing the shadow's face. Moments later, a blade was driven through its chest.

Zarrow looked up to the sky. At the moon, bathed in a shimmering, pale light. "Shit," he muttered. "Shit, shit, shit. Kaurazi!" He hobbled toward the village center, damning the searing sensation traveling up his leg. "*KAURAZI!*"

He continued to scream his friend's name until his voice was hoarse with fear and anger. The village was erupting into an orgy of blood and madness. Thirteen Eclipseborn had remained hereat the night's start after Tabrum's passing. He could not say how many still remained.

The air had already succumbed to the horrid stench of death. And the villagers had succumbed to the bloodlust from which it resulted.

As he ran as far as his injured legs would take him, Zarrow watched Tribespeople roaming the pathways, so many of them brandishing something that could be fashioned as a weapon, whether blunt or edged. They all ran off in directions they surmised to be the location of an Eclipseborn, chanting for their lives, promising to fulfill the gods' wishes. Zarrow wove in and out of the way of several of them, knocking some to the ground, facing their ire but ignoring them just the same. There was nothing he could do for those who were being chased. Nothing he could do except save Kaurazi.

"Get away from me!" a voice shrilly rang out nearby.

"I know that voice," Zarrow muttered. He followed the sound of the voice, which was accompanied by forceful grunts and snarls.

"Unhand me!"

"Shut your mouth, girl! This shall be over quickly!"

Zarrow broke into a sprint, adrenaline roaring through him, eliminating all the residual pain in his body. As he turned a corner, he saw feet dangling, the voice screaming, the sound of steel scraping against a whetstone. Ceverra was strung up at the wrists, a line of rope tied around a tree branch like a pulley. Before her stood one of the shamans, still readying his blade.

Ceverra's eyes shot open wide as she caught sight of Zarrow. "Help me! Zarrow, please! Zarrow!"

The shaman did not even show a cursory glance toward Zarrow. "It is too late, girl." And he drove the blade through Ceverra's stomach. Once, twice, thrice, four times.

"No!" Zarrow screamed. He charged and tackled the shaman to the ground, rolling in the dirt with him as Ceverra's blood poured down upon them. Zarrow had the shaman's blade hand pinned, but the man's free hand reached up toward Zarrow's face, finding his eyes, trying to claw at them but only raking at the skin underneath.

Zarrow growled and brought a heavy knee down to the man's groin, stealing away his breath. The blade fell from the shaman's hands, and Zarrow found his opportunity. In a swift movement, he deftly picked up the steel, slicing at the bastard's wrist in the process. He held the weapon up high, point facing down, and drove it through the shaman's throat with enough force that it came out the other end and through the earth below.

He winced through the newfound pain to his face, the claw marks forming bloody valleys in his cheek, which filled with the red rain from above as Ceverra, still dangling from the tree branch, managed to meekly whimper, her lips and chin already slickened with a crimson stain.

Exerting as much effort as he could manage, Zarrow pulled the blade out from the sheath of the shaman's throat and jumped as high as he could to cut the rope above Ceverra's wrists. It took three tries to slice all the way through, but when he finally did so, she fell helplessly to the ground, hardly any strength remaining in her at all.

"Shit, shit, come on, stay with me, Ceverra," Zarrow said, turning her over onto her back. Blood was gushing from the four stab wounds. He pressed down on her stomach, the act met with meek protest on Ceverra's part, but no matter how much pressure Zarrow placed, the blood continued to stream through the slits of his fingers.

He glanced at her as her eyes began glossing over, a tear falling down the side of her face. Ceverra looked back to Zarrow as though she were about to say something, but she could no longer form words. She offered two final shallow breaths, weakly shook her head, and then closed her eyes.

Zarrow felt frozen. Slowly, he lifted his bloodied hands from Ceverra's lifeless form, raising them to his forehead in a silent prayer. He knew not to whom or to what he should pray. It was not within his purview to know what the gods spoke or wished. Why should it be within his purview to offer to them his prayers for the departed?

All that was within him to do was lean back on his heels and watch her soul leave this world. Even as hell continued to rage about him. Even as the night air was rife with the sound of cold steel meeting hot flesh, of piercing screams begging for mercy, of footsteps marching along the pathways, hunting for the remaining Eclipseborn as though they were beasts reduced to quarry.

And of the silence marked by one set of footsteps stopped in its tracks.

"Ceverra...?" spoke the familiar voice, calm yet undertones of shock coating the words. "Z...Zarrow? What did you..."

Tears trickled down Zarrow's face as he turned to at last find Kaurazi, appearing worse for wear but otherwise and, most importantly, still alive. His clothing was scorched and drenched in blood, his face and arms littered with slashes and scrapes, a red-stained hunter's knife brandished in his hand.

"K...K...Kaurazi..." Zarrow muttered. Everything hurt. His body, his soul, his pride. It hurt just to say words at all.

Kaurazi took two tentative steps forward, craning his head past his friend to glance at Ceverra's dead body. He clenched his eyes shut, biting his lower lip, tightening his grip on the blade. "What've you done, Zarrow?" he asked softly.

Zarrow looked at his own trembling hands, still fresh with Ceverra's blood. He frowned as tears welled in his eyes. "No," he whispered. "It...it wasn't..."

"Told you this would happen, Zarrow." Kaurazi held the blade out, keeping Zarrow at arm's length. "It's always gonna be us. They were just lookin' for a reason. Just didn't think you'd've found that reason, too."

Furiously, Zarrow shook his head. "I didn't…" He clenched his eyes shut, damming up the tears. "Godsdamn it, Kaurazi, I tried to stop it, but I—"

"But you didn't."

"Not for lack of trying." *And damn it, did I try.*

Kaurazi looked around, seeming to listen to the carnage throughout the village. "And look at where your effort has led us."

Zarrow sank into the earth, digging his nails through the dirt, the soil soaking up the remains of Ceverra's blood. He had nothing to say. He had nothing he *could* say.

"Stand up, Zarrow."

His eyes shot up, disbelieving that the words came from Kaurazi's mouth. He was still holding the blade out towards him. "Kaurazi, what are you—"

"I don't have a say in this," Kaurazi said, his voice cracking, his lip shaking. "Neither should you."

"Kaurazi…" Zarrow held his hands out, placating his friend to stop. "We don't have to do this. Don't *make* me do this."

Kaurazi pointed to the blood still dripping from Zarrow's hands. "*That's* why I have to do this."

"I'm trying to tell you, I wasn't the one who—"

"It doesn't matter, Zarrow!" Kaurazi bellowed. "It *never* matters for us Eclipseborn! There's never gonna be a place for me, never gonna be a place for the Eclipseborn! You *saw* what would happen, and still, you did nothin' to stop it!"

I saw all of this, Zarrow thought, agreeing. *And one more thing is still to come.*

Kaurazi's eyes were red and puffy with tears. He drew in a deep breath, steeling himself. "I've accepted I'm not makin' it past tonight. So, if there's a hand to end me…I'd rather it's yours."

Zarrow unsteadily rose to his feet, gripping the shaman's discarded blade beside him. "You could run. Far from here."

"And where would I go, Zarrow? Where would any of us go?"

The blade quivered in Zarrow's hand. "I wish I knew," he admitted.

Slowly, Kaurazi nodded his head. "And that is why it must be this way." He crouched, ready to pounce. "Thank you, my friend. For everything."

Zarrow wiped away a tear with the back of his hand, feeling the smear of blood coat his face. "I'm sorry, Kaurazi." He didn't know what else he could say.

There was nothing in Kaurazi's face suggesting he was ready to forgive. There was no repentance for this night. Zarrow knew that. He didn't actively participate in this heinous night, but he killed just the same.

And when Kaurazi launched forward, blade drawn, Zarrow could only do as his instincts ordered him.

Survive.

The blades sang their song of war and battle as they met, steel scraping against steel. Zarrow assumed a defensive position, blocking each of Kaurazi's telegraphed maneuvers. Neither of them was a fighter. The Dusk Tribe did not breed or train for extensive combat. But Zarrow knew enough about when to stand firm...

And when to strike back.

Kaurazi brought his blade down with a two-handed strike, but Zarrow moved within his guard, grasping his friend's wrists, pulling them apart, prying loose the steel until it fell to the ground. In response, Kaurazi based his forehead into Zarrow's nose, the move stunning the recipient. Zarrow saw stars flash in his vision, but it did not prevent him from holding tightly to his weapon, even as Kaurazi moved to steal it from his grasp.

The battle immediately became for the blade. They both held the hilt with two hands, each digging their feet in as they tried to guide the end to its target. It was a tug-of-war, neither giving an inch. Zarrow grimaced as the adrenaline gradually began to wear off, the flaming fury within his leg making a grand return. But the pain also restored his focus, reinvigorated him, and as he caught his second wind, the blade inched closer and closer to Kaurazi's chest. And slowly...

Slowly...

Steel found flesh.

Kaurazi's breathing sputtered as Zarrow tearfully pushed the blade deeper into his friend's chest, right up to the crossguard. Blood poured around the handle as Kaurazi's grip slackened, his knees buckling. Zarrow caught him as he fell backward, lifting him to his knees.

The two friends looked at each other, matching glares, Zarrow unsure what to make of what dwelt within Kaurazi's eyes. Sorrow, most of all, surely. Anger, solace, regret?

Regret was certainly what glinted in his own eyes. How could he not regret these circumstances as they passed? But sorrow, as well. A deep, painful sorrow. Zarrow had assuredly lost much this night. But for his friend, his closest friend?

What little he had, Kaurazi had lost it all.

They exchanged no words. Zarrow simply laid Kaurazi down on the ground, gently placing his head upon the earth. It was not much longer until Kaurazi closed his eyes. And did not open them again.

Chaos continued to reign off in the background. Fires rippled and roared, a beacon certainly visible from miles upon miles away. But Zarrow could hardly bring himself to move. Once he left...he knew that was it. The deed was done. The threads of fate were not so easily unwoven. And this moment, whether preordained by the gods or not, had him woven deep within its loom.

He placed a hand atop Kaurazi's slick forehead, whispering a wordless apology, and rose back to his feet. Solemnly, he turned and limped away from his friend, tears flowing down his blood- and dust-stained cheeks. The raucous night raged on deeper in the village, but Zarrow had no intention of looking upon it.

He made his way toward the village borders to the north, where all remained as it should have been. Quiet, peaceful, tranquil. But when he spared a final glance at his home, he found it bathed in the light of the pale moon, the trails and puddles of blood shimmering in that glow, almost unnaturally. It seemed...sinister, even. It sent a chill down Zarrow's spine. A chill he could no longer indulge.

As the rank stench of acrid smoke and death filled his nostrils, Zarrow turned and walked away from it all, towards a pristine land not so fatally obsessed with death.

If only his first steps had not stained that beautiful green field with shades of red.

EPILOGUE

THE RED FIELDS

It was not for Zarrow to say how long he had wandered the fields to the north. He couldn't even say with any certainty how far he had traveled or if he was simply roaming about in circles.

All he knew was that the moon had not moved from its position the entire night. Almost as though it was watching the village. Almost as though it was watching *him.*

The pale light still shimmered overhead, bathing the fertile land-scape in an ethereal glow, illuminating the way with no need for torchlight. It was convenient and yet unsettling just the same.

Something tugged at him as he looked skyward. Like a weight was pressing down upon him. Not just that: like something was *pulling* at him from down below. When Zarrow looked to his feet, he found nothing.

But the *feeling* remained. The sensation never disappeared. *Something* was there with him, but he couldn't precisely say what.

"Off to find a new place to go after all, aren't you?"

Zarrow's heart jumped, unaware that anyone was following him. He spun around, a surge of pain jumping up his leg in so doing.

But there was no one there.

"Was this part of what you saw, as well, Zarrow?"

Zarrow looked from side to side, his heart pounding. "That voice…" His eyes widened. "Kaurazi…?"

Kaurazi's voice chuckled. "Seems the shamans got what they wanted after all. Wonder if the rest of the Tribe will welcome it. Or maybe it's a curse, after all."

He shook his head back and forth. "No, no, no, this isn't real." Zarrow clenched his eyes shut. "This can't be happening, no, no, no."

A grunt echoed in Zarrow's ear. "Are you so upset to hear my voice again already, Zarrow? Or were you hoping to run away from the consequences?"

"Get out of my head! This isn't real!"

"It is," Kaurazi's voice said plainly. "Didn't have to be, but it is."

Zarrow gasped, his chest growing tighter. Everything the shamans…his father…everything they strove to accomplish. It really happened. They got their wish in the end.

But as he looked up at the shining moon, he could swear he heard laughter. Haunting, sinister laughter.

None of it felt like an accomplishment. It felt like…

Like a…

A CURSE.

Zarrow shuddered the more he glanced at the moon. Because the longer he stared, the longer he felt as though it had spoken to him. And the only word it spoke was:

CURSE.

And laughter followed with it.

A Message for the Reader

If you've made it this far: you have my heartfelt thanks for reading PALE NIGHT, RED FIELDS.

If it's not too much to ask, I would very much appreciate you giving a quick review of PALE NIGHT, RED FIELDS on Goodreads and/or Amazon. Reviews are incredibly important for authors (and indie authors especially!) as they enable us to expand our reach and let more and more potential readers know that our books exist! And on top of that, I would love to hear your thoughts on this book, regardless of whether they are good or bad, and I hope to see you again for the next book.

Thank you,
Joe

ACKNOWLEDGMENTS

As always, my first heartfelt thanks extends to you, the reader. Without you, I would just be screaming words at myself and probably getting thrown out of Wal-Mart for causing a scene. Thanks for saving us all from that.

To my dear friends Adam Maguire and Samantha Smith, I am always grateful to you both. You've instilled in me the courage to pursue this path, and given me the assurance that there will always be an audience for my writing – even if it might only just be the two of you.

To all my friends in the Indie Accords Discord server, you help make navigating this whole indie publishing thing so much less stressful. In all of you, I have a boundless resource for all of my questions, even if I feel too embarrassed to ask them. You're all wonderful. (Even you, Thiago. I'm eating some raisins as I write this, though.)

And, of course, to my beloved Annie: you give me the confidence to pursue anything I set my mind to. You may not always understand what the hell I'm talking about when I pitch ideas to you, but you always give me your support, regardless. Our robot vacuum son Crumb and I are lucky to have you.

Joseph John Lee is the author of The Spellbinders and the Gunslingers trilogy. A true product of New England, he prefers Dunkin' over Starbucks, sometimes speaks with a Boston accent, and does not say the word "wicked" in casual conversation as much as one may think. He currently lives in Boston with his fiancé, Annie, and their robot vacuum named Crumb.

* 9 7 9 8 9 8 6 3 8 3 3 6 1 *